I Wish Wish Wish Wish for you

Words by

Sandra Magsamen

Pictures by

MELISA FERNÁNDEZ NITSCHE

sourcebooks
wonderland

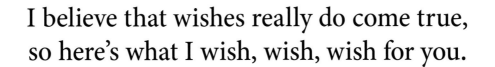

I believe that wishes really do come true,
so here's what I wish, wish, wish for you.

I wish that you find beauty
in ordinary things

like the sunrise, the mountains,
and butterfly wings.

I wish that you laugh and laugh and laugh out loud

and that you know how it feels to feel really proud.

I wish that when you look at the stars
that glow and twinkle at night

you'll know that you are part of it all,
and you too shine bright.

I wish that you will always know
that on the other side of sad

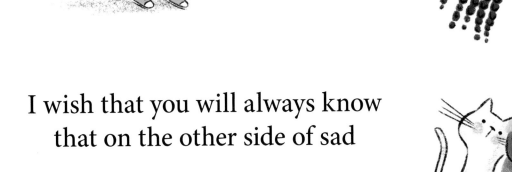

there are many more moments
where you'll feel glad.

I wish that your adventures take you far and wide
and that you never pass up a wild and fun ride!

I wish that you try many things that are new
and that you learn there's nothing
you can't do!

I wish you way more *do*s than *don't*s

and lots more *I will*s than *I won't*s.

I wish that your dreams take you very far

and that you always stay true to who you are.

I wish that you make friends
who believe in you

and that you are a good friend to them too.

I wish that lots of sunshine
and smiles fill each day

and when it rains you look for
rainbows as you play.

I wish that you come to know that kindness
is always the best choice

and that you always speak from your heart
when you use your voice.

I wish that you see the strengths
in people who are different than you

and that you stand up for equality, fairness, and justice too!

I wish you everything and so much more.

I wish you all the beauty that life has in store.

But most of all the biggest wish that
I wish, wish, wish for you

is that you know I will love you
always and forever too!

To my daughter, Hannah, and to all the sons and daughters on our planet.
May this book be a gentle reminder to believe in wishes, to believe in hope,
to believe in each other, and to believe each of us makes a difference in the world.
I believe wishes are like stars…you don't always see them,
but you know they are always there.

— SM

To my parents, who wished everything for me.

— MFN

Published by Sourcebooks Wonderland, an imprint of Sourcebooks Kids
P.O. Box 4410, Naperville, Illinois 60567–4410
(630) 961-3900
sourcebookskids.com

Library of Congress Cataloging-in-Publication Data is on file with the publisher.

Source of Production: Worzalla, Stevens Point, Wisconsin, United States of America
Date of Production: October 2021
Run Number: 5023110

Printed and bound in the United States of America.
WOZ 10 9 8 7 6 5 4 3 2 1

Note from the Author

Big heartfelt thanks to Karen Botti and Hannah Magsamen Barry. Their creativity and generous spirits are unique and valued gifts to me and the work we create in the studio. Without Sourcebooks, my wish to create this book would not have come true. I'm grateful for the support, expertise, and love from Dominique Raccah, Karen Shapiro, Nicky Benson, Taylor Maccoux, Brittany Vibbert, Jordan Kost, and all the others who touch my books. Thank you, Melisa Fernández Nitsche, for your stunning illustrations that brought this book to life.

Note from the Illustrator

Thank you so much to my agent, Chad W. Beckerman, for his guidance and advice. Thank you to Christy Ewers at the CAT Agency for letting me be a part of the most amazing group of artists. You both have changed my life forever and made my dream come true. To Sandra Magsamen, thank you for allowing me to illustrate your beautiful words! Eternally grateful that I got to be a part of this project and for *I Wish, Wish, Wish for You* to be my first picture book. It was an incredible experience. Thank you to Brittany Vibbert, and the entire Sourcebooks team that worked on this book, for trusting me and my vision. Thank you to my friend Sol Cotti for encouraging me to show my work.